P9-DDS-801

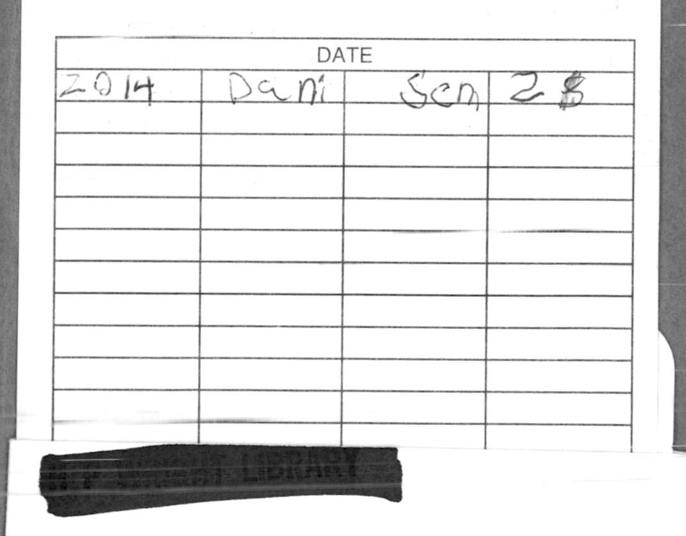
DATE

Troll Teacher

By VIVIAN VANDE VELDE
Illustrated by MARY JANE AUCH

Holiday House/New York

Elizabeth noticed right away that her new teacher was a troll.

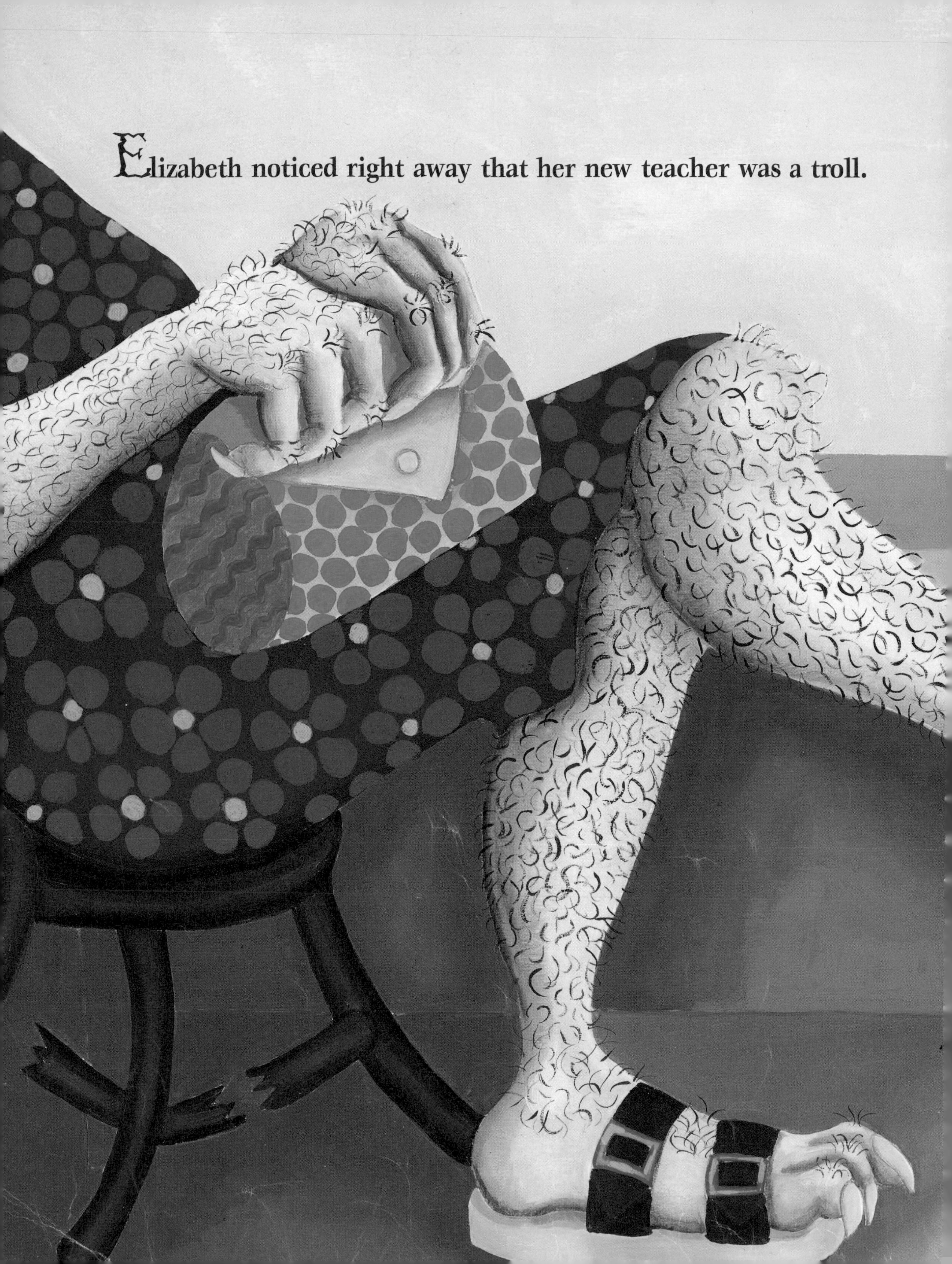

OFFICE
MR. BOYNIK
PRINCIPAL

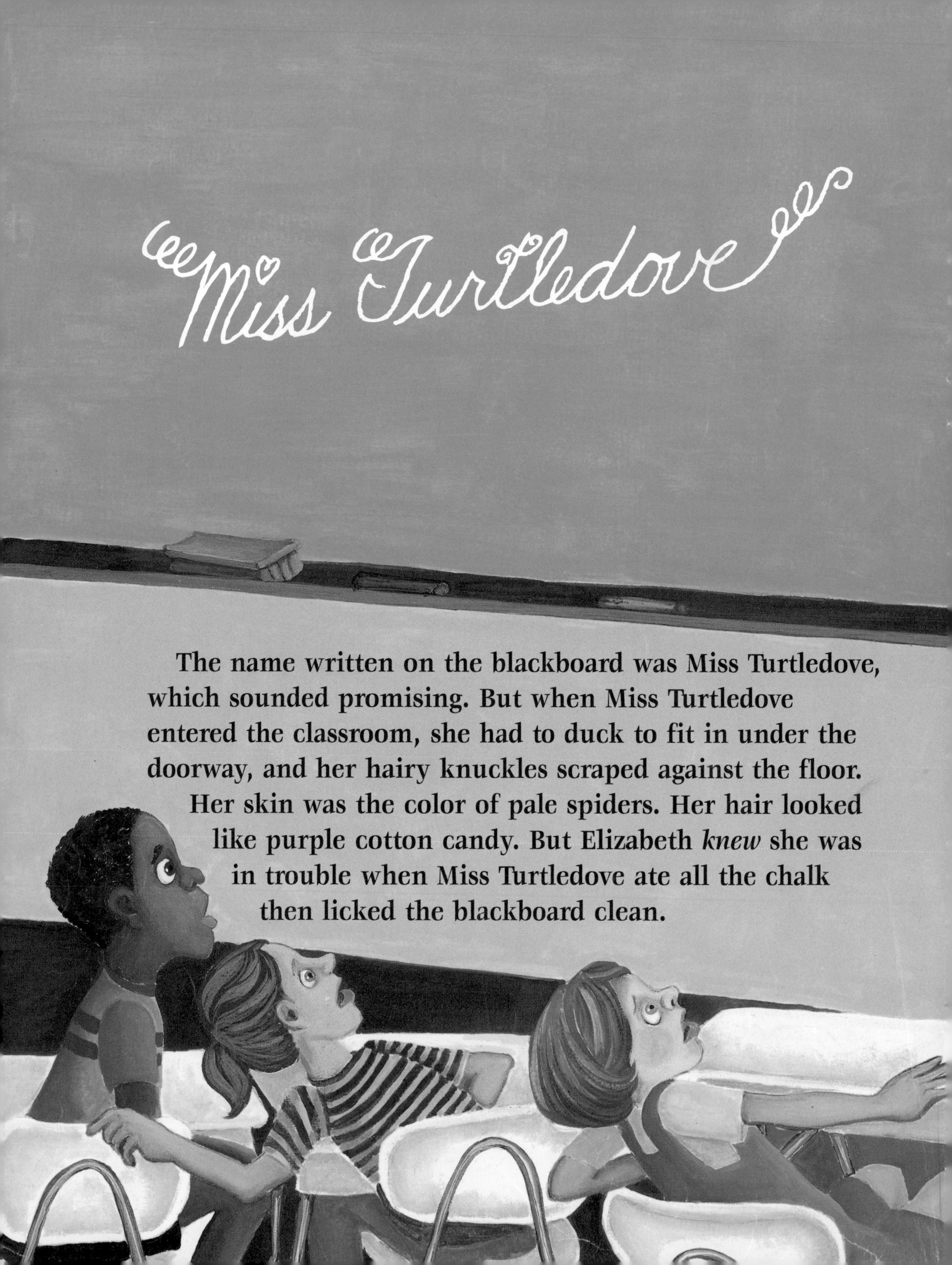

The name written on the blackboard was Miss Turtledove, which sounded promising. But when Miss Turtledove entered the classroom, she had to duck to fit in under the doorway, and her hairy knuckles scraped against the floor. Her skin was the color of pale spiders. Her hair looked like purple cotton candy. But Elizabeth *knew* she was in trouble when Miss Turtledove ate all the chalk then licked the blackboard clean.

Elizabeth sank down in her chair and tried to hide behind Nicholas.

"Now children," said Miss Turtledove, tapping her long, sharp pointer stick against her warty palm. "Pay attention. Two plus two equals seventeen. Except on Tuesdays, when they're thirty-two."

Elizabeth sank lower in her seat.

"The capital of New York State is Bolivia."

Elizabeth sank even lower in her seat.

"George Washington invented pizza in 1954."

Elizabeth sank so low in her seat that she fell out of her chair.

Miss Turtledove stared at Elizabeth. "If you must sit on the floor," she said, "move your desk to the cloakroom where it won't be in the way."

By the end of the day, the cloakroom was cluttered with three other desks, as well as the class aquarium, the wall clock, and a picture of Mr. Boynik, the principal.

Love,
Mr. P.

"My teacher is a troll," Elizabeth told her brother, Tony, on the bus ride home.

"*Your* teacher!" he answered. "First day of school and *my* teacher's already assigned a book report."

"My teacher is a troll," Elizabeth told her mother, who had just come home from work.

"Gee, that's too bad," her mother said, handing Elizabeth the silverware and plates to set the table.

"My teacher is a troll," Elizabeth told her father at dinner.

"That's not nice," her father said. "Where do you get that?" He glared at Tony. "Where does she get that sort of thing?"

Tony shrugged.

The next day at school, Miss Turtledove said it was art day, but she made the children hold the crayons in their teeth. When Dawn drew a house, Miss Turtledove said that was rude and sent her to the principal's office.

Gloria insisted she didn't know where to put the letter "x" in the word "shoe," and she got sent to the office, too.

And Terry was sent there for looking too neat during recess.

By the end of the day, there were seven children sent to Mr. Boynik's office, and five more desks in the cloakroom. Miss Turtledove told the children to shape up or she'd run her fingernails down the blackboard.

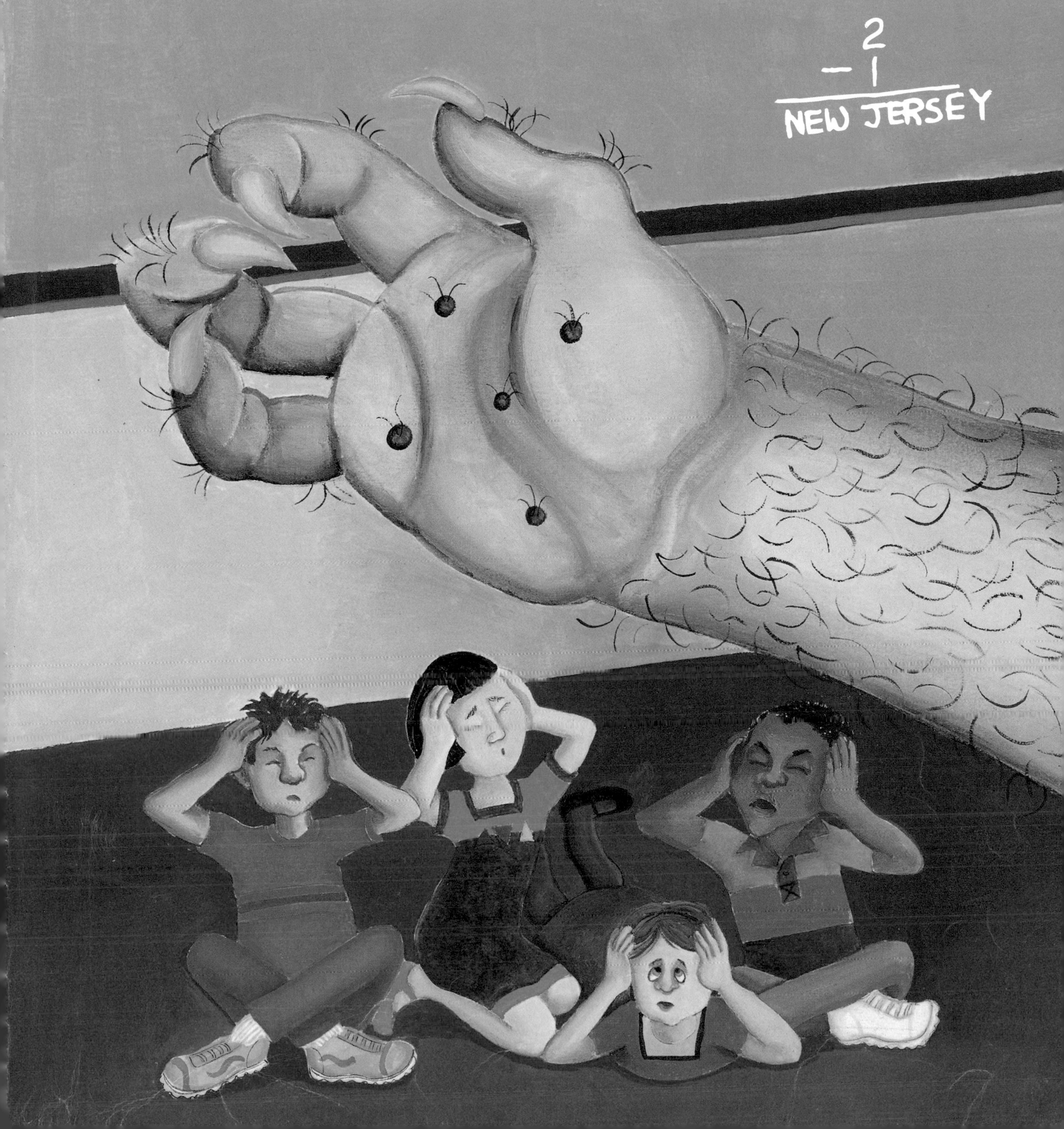

That evening, parents and students and teachers were invited to a Get Together Ice Cream Social.

Now they'll see, Elizabeth thought.

But her parents didn't see. Parents never do.

Miss Turtledove stood there in the orange dress that matched her eyes but showed her hairy knees. She smiled at the parents, all her pointy teeth gleaming. "Such a sweet child," she said about each of the children, all the while tapping her pointer against her warty palm. "A pleasure to have in my class."

"Did you see?" Elizabeth asked, tugging on her father's sleeve. "Did you see she's a troll?"

"Quiet," said her father, as Mr. Boynik, the principal, came up to them. "Where does she get that?" he whispered to Elizabeth's mother, who shrugged.

"An excellent teacher," Mr. Boynik told them, "that Miss Turtledove."

"Yes, we can see," said Elizabeth's parents, smiling.

"Lucky we could get her," Mr. Boynik said.

"Lucky indeed," her parents agreed, nodding.

"And so pretty and pleasant," Mr. Boynik said. "You're a lucky girl, Lizzie." Mr. Boynik patted Elizabeth on the head.

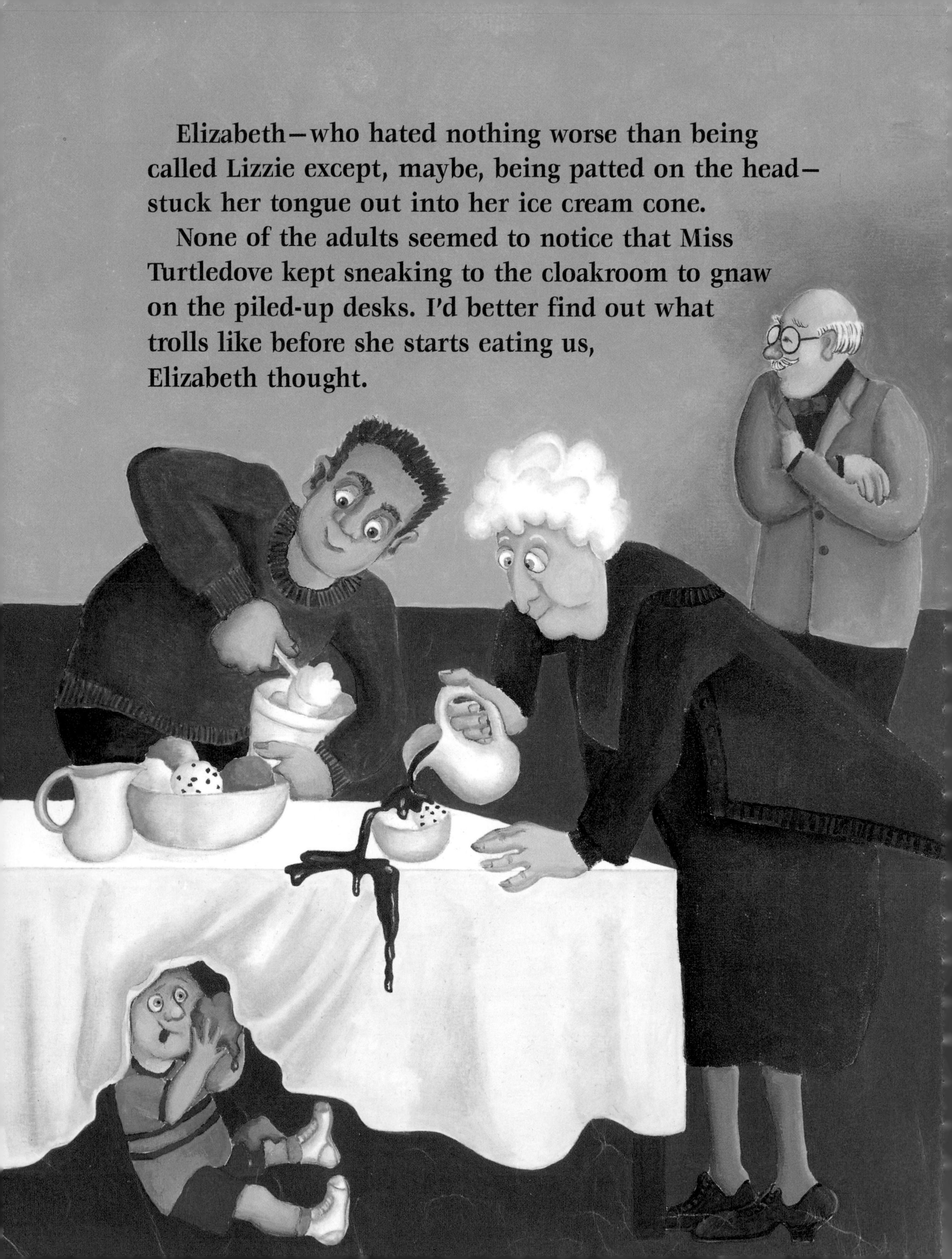

Elizabeth—who hated nothing worse than being called Lizzie except, maybe, being patted on the head—stuck her tongue out into her ice cream cone.

None of the adults seemed to notice that Miss Turtledove kept sneaking to the cloakroom to gnaw on the piled-up desks. I'd better find out what trolls like before she starts eating us, Elizabeth thought.

The next day, while Miss Turtledove was in the cloakroom eating backpacks, Elizabeth put a valentine on the teacher's desk—even though she was either five months early or seven months late. She didn't sign the card since Miss Turtledove had never asked the children their names anyway. Elizabeth just wrote: "Your Friend." Surely even a troll wouldn't eat a friend.

But when Miss Turtledove came back into the room, she ate the card.

Still, she must have liked the gift: she threw hardly any blackboard erasers at the children that morning.

She'll eat anything, Elizabeth thought. Well, not exactly anything. Several of the children had tried giving her apples and oranges and bananas, and she'd just used those to throw at the students.

She'll eat anything that's uneatable, Elizabeth thought.

So the following day, Elizabeth brought in one of her brother's old gym socks, and she put that on Miss Turtledove's desk.

As soon as Miss Turtledove came in, she began munching away on the sock.

Just then, Mr. Boynik stuck his head in the door and asked, "Did you see what I left you?"

He was pointing at a pile of papers on her desk, but Miss Turtledove hadn't seen that. She'd only seen the sock.

She gave a cry of joy and ran over to hug him, the toe of the sock still hanging between her teeth.

"Miss Turtledove, really!" Mr. Boynik said. "Not in front of the children!"

Miss Turtledove picked him up and flung him over her shoulder and ran out the door.

The last the children saw of them was through the window. Miss Turtledove was running across the baseball field, still carrying Mr. Boynik. The principal's voice could still be heard, very faintly, his tiny voice saying, "Miss Turtledove! Really! Miss Turtledove!"

MR. SCHMIDLOPP
~~VICE~~ PRINCIPAL

School was dismissed early that day, though none of the adults would ever admit that the teacher had been a troll. The vice principal said a substitute teacher would come the next day. He assured them that she was an excellent teacher, as well as being pretty and pleasant, and they were very lucky to get her.

To all the teachers who aren't trolls
V. V. V. and M. J. A.

Printed in the United States of America
First Edition

The art for this book was prepared with water soluble oil paint
on coated watercolor paper.

The book type was set in Veljovic Bold.

Library of Congress Cataloging-in-Publication Data

Vande Velde, Vivian.
Troll teacher / by Vivian Vande Velde; illustrated by Mary Jane Auch.—1st ed.
p. cm.
Summary: Elizabeth tries to tell her family that there is
something wrong with her new teacher, but they cannot see it,
even though Miss Turtledove has orange eyes,
eats desks, and throws fruit at the students.
ISBN 0-8234-1503-1 (hardcover)
[1. Teachers—Fiction. 2. Schools—Fiction. 3. Trolls—Fiction.]
I. Auch, Mary Jane, ill. II. Title.
PZ7.V377 Tr 2000
[E]—dc21 00-026796